Stir

Megan McDonald

illustrated by

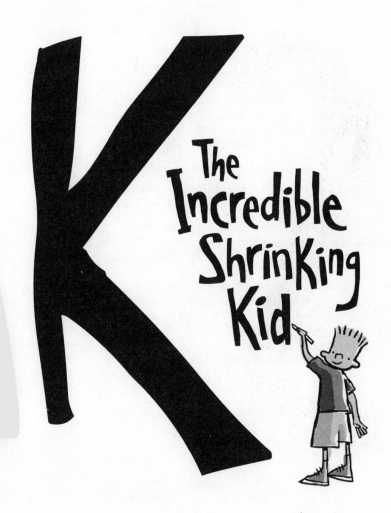

K

The
Incredible
Shrinking
Kid

Peter H. Reynolds

CANDLEWICK PRESS
CAMBRIDGE, MASSACHUSETTS

First paperback edition 2006

The Library of Congress has cataloged
the hardcover edition as follows:

McDonald, Megan.
Stink : the incredible shrinking kid / Megan McDonald ; illustrated by
Peter H. Reynolds. — 1st ed.
p. cm.
Summary: The shortest kid in the second grade, James Moody, also
known as Stink, learns all about the shortest president of the United
States, James Madison, when they celebrate Presidents' Day at school.
ISBN 0-7636-2025-4 (hardcover)
[1. Size—Fiction. 2. Schools—Fiction. 3. Brothers and sisters—Fiction.
4. Presidents—Fiction.] I. Reynolds, Peter, ill. II. Title.
PZ7.M478419St 2005
[Fic]—dc22   2003065246

ISBN 0-7636-2891-3 (paperback)

2 4 6 8 10 9 7 5 3 1

Printed in the United States of America

The book was typeset in Stone Informal.
The illustrations were created digitally.

Candlewick Press
2067 Massachusetts Avenue
Cambridge, Massachusetts 02140

visit us at www.candlewick.com

for all the readers who asked for Stink
M. M.

To the Gary Stager, members of the
Multimedia House of Pancakes, and
every Hotdog-on-a-Stick employee
past, present, and future.
P. H. R.

CONTENTS

SHORT,

SHORTER,

SHORTEST

Shrimp-o!

Runtsville!

Shorty Pants!

Stink was short. Short, shorter, shortest. Short as an inchworm. Short as a . . . stinkbug!

Stink was the shortest one in the Moody family (except for Mouse, the cat). The shortest second-grader in Class 2D. Probably the shortest human being in the whole world, *including Alaska and Hawaii.* Stink was one whole head shorter than his sister, Judy Moody. Every morning he made Judy measure him. And every morning it was the same.

Three feet, eight inches tall.

Shrimpsville.

He had not grown one inch. Not one centimeter. Not one hair.

He was always one head shorter than Judy. "I need another head," he told his mom and dad.

"What for?" asked Dad.

"I like your head just the way it is," said Mom.

"You need a new *brain*," said Judy.

"I have to get taller," said Stink. "How can I get taller?"

"Eat your peas," said Dad.

"Drink your milk," said Mom.

"Eat more seafood!" said Judy.

"Seafood?"

"Yes—*shrimp*!" Judy said.

"Hardee-har-har," said Stink. His sister thought she was so funny.

"What's so bad about being short?" asked Dad.

"I have to drink at the baby fountain," said Stink. "And stand in the front row for class pictures. And I always have to be a mouse in school plays," said Stink. "Just once, I'd like a speaking part, not a *squeaking* part."

"Being short isn't all bad," said Dad. "You still get those free coloring books you like at the doctor's."

"And the Spider-Man pajamas you love still fit you," said Mom.

"And you still get to use your baby step stool just to brush your teeth," said Judy. Stink rolled his eyes.

"You'll grow," said Dad.

"Growing takes time," said Mom.

"Lie down on the floor," Judy told him.

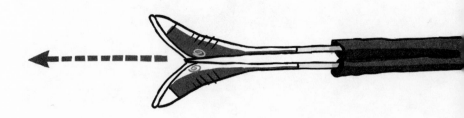

"What for?"

"If I pull your arms, and Mom and Dad each take a leg, we could stretch you out like a rubber band. Then you'd be taller."

Stink did not want to be a rubber band. So he ate all his peas at dinner. He did not hide even one in his napkin. He drank all his milk, and did not pour even one drop into Judy's glass when she wasn't looking.

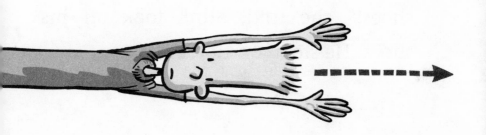

* * *

"Measure me again," Stink said to Judy. "One more time. Before bed."

"Stink, I just measured you this morning."

"That was before I ate all those peas and drank all that milk," said Stink.

Stink put on his shoes. He stood next to the Shrimp-O-Meter. He stood up straight. He stood up tall.

Judy got out her Elizabeth Blackwell Women of Science ruler. "Hey, no shoes!" she said. Stink took off his shoes. He stood on tiptoe.

"No tippy-toes either."

Judy measured Stink top to bottom. She measured him foot to head. She measured him head to foot. Something was not right.

"Well?" asked Stink.

"Bad news," said Judy.

"What?" asked Stink.

"You're shorter than you were this morning. One quarter inch shorter!"

Stink made a face. "Not possible."

"Stink. The Women of Science ruler does not lie."

"Shorter? How can I be shorter?"

"Simple," said Judy. "You shrunk!"

"You'll grow," said Dad.

"You'll grow," said Mom.

"But you'll never, ever, *ever* catch up to me!" said Judy.

The Adventures of Stink
in Shrink Monster

BY STINK MOODY

The horrible Shrink Monster attacks the City of Moodyville!

ZAP!

EEEEK!

BEFORE

ZAP!

AFTER

Stink, the bravest (and shortest) kid in Moodyville, confronts the Shrink Monster!

GRRRRRR!

STOP!

ZAP

Huh?

Stink shrunk!

Max, fetch the Stink-Mobile.

Good boy, Max.

Will Stink have enough time to invent an un-shrinker? Or will Stink be attending Molecule Elementary School?

StinK-Mobile

SHRINK, SHRANK, SHRUNK

When Stink woke up the next morning, his bed felt as big as a country. The ceiling was up there with the sky. And it was a long way down to the floor.

When he went to brush his teeth, even the sink seemed too tall.

"Yipe! I really am shrinking," said Stink, checking himself out in the mirror. Were his arms a little shorter? Was his head a little smaller?

Stink got dressed. He put on up-and-down-striped pants and an up-and-down-striped shirt.

"What's with the stripes?" asked Judy.

"Makes me look taller," said Stink.

"If you say so," said Judy.

"What?"

"If you really want to look taller, here's what you do." Judy handed him a fancy shampoo-type bottle. "Put this hair gel on your hair and leave it in for ten minutes. Then you'll be able to comb your hair so it sticks straight up. Sticking-up hair will make you look taller."

Stink put the goopy goop in his hair. He left it in his hair while he made his bed. He left it in his hair while he packed up his backpack. He left it in his hair all through breakfast.

"We could play baseball, and you could be *short*stop," Judy told him.

"So funny I forgot to laugh," said Stink.

Judy pointed to Stink's hair. "Hey, I think it's working!" she said.

"Really? Do you think people will notice?"

"They'll notice," said Judy.

Stink ran upstairs to look in the mirror. "HEY! My HAIR! It's ORANGE!"

"Don't worry," said Judy. "It'll wash out . . . in about a week."

"I look like a carrot!" said Stink.

"Carrots are tall," said Judy, and she laughed all the way to the bus stop.

Stink's friend Elizabeth sat next to him in class. They were the shortest kids in Class 2D, so they sat up front. "Hi, Elizabeth," said Stink.

"I'm not Elizabeth anymore," she told Stink. "From now on, call me Sophie of the Elves."

"Okay. I have a new name, too. The Incredible Shrinking Stink."

"But, Stink, you look taller today," said Elizabeth.

"It's just the hair," said Stink. "I'm still short."

"Not to an elf. To an elf, you'd be a giant. To an elf, you would be the Elf King."

"Thanks, Sophie of the Elves," said Stink.

The bell rang, and Mrs. Dempster passed out spelling words. Three of the new words were *shrink, shrank, shrunk.* At lunch, the dessert was strawberry *short*cake. And in Reading, Mrs. Dempster read everybody a book called *The Shrinking of Treehorn.*

The book was all about a boy who plays games and reads cereal boxes and gets shorter and shorter. He keeps shrinking and shrinking. Then, just when he becomes a normal size again, he turns green!

"Any comments?" Mrs. Dempster asked when the story was over.

Stink raised his hand. "Is that a true story?"

Mrs. D. laughed. "I'm afraid not," she said. "It's fantasy."

"Fantasy's my favorite!" said Sophie of the Elves. "Especially hobbits and elves."

"Are you sure it's fantasy?" asked Stink. "Because that kid is a lot like me. Because I'm . . . I'm . . ." Stink could not make himself say *shrinking*.

"Because you both turned another color?" asked Webster.

"Um, because I like to read everything on the cereal box, too," said Stink.

"Okay," said Mrs. Dempster. "Let's see. Who's going to carry the milk from the cafeteria today?" Stink was barely paying attention. He never got asked to carry the milk.

"How about Mr. James Moody?" asked Mrs. Dempster.

"Me?" asked Stink. He sat up taller. "I get to carry the milk?"

Stink walked down the second-grade hallway. It looked longer than usual. And wider. He took the stairs down to the cafeteria. Were there always this many stairs? His legs felt shorter. Like they shrink, shrank, shrunk.

Stink got the milk crate. He carried the milk up the stairs, past the office, and past the teachers' room. Now his arms felt shorter. He needed a rest. He set the milk down outside the nurse's office.

"Hi, Stink!" called Mrs. Bell. "I see you have a new hairstyle."

"My sister turned it ORANGE," said Stink.

"So, what brings you here today? Headache? Sore throat? There's a lot going around, you know."

"Is shrinking going around?" asked Stink. "Because I think I'm shrinking.

As in getting shorter."

"You're shrinking? What makes you think so?"

"My sister. I mean, she measures me every morning. And I'm always three feet, eight inches. But last night she measured me before I went to bed, and I'd shrunk! I was only three feet, seven and three quarters inches. I'm a whole quarter inch shorter!"

"Don't worry, honey," said Mrs. Bell. "Everybody shrinks during the day. We're all a little shorter at night than we are in the morning."

"Seriously?"

"Seriously. From gravity, and all the walking around we do, the pads between our bones shrink during the day. At night they soak up water and expand again."

"We all shrink?" asked Stink.

"That's what I'm saying. Everybody shrinks."

"Scientific!" said Stink.

The Adventures of Stink
in King of the Elves

BY STINK MOODY

Beautiful Sophie of the Elves falls under the dreaded gravity spell.

An evil witch pours hex-mix in Sophie's sneakers.

My feet feel sooo HEAVY...

POOF!

TA-DA!
STINK, King of the ELVES, arrives!
Not a minute to lose!

ANTI-GRAVITY SOAKING CHAMBER
1 MILE →

THERE!

30 SECONDS LATER...
My hero!

A Larger-than-life statue to thank you, Stink!
STINK King of the ELVES

UP,

UP,

UP

Stink walked tall down the hall, around the corner, and back to class 2D.

"Stink! You won!" said Sophie of the Elves.

"While you were gone," said Mrs. Dempster, "we drew a name to see who would get to take Newton home this weekend. Your name was chosen."

"For real? Me? I get to take the newt home?"

"You have all the luck," said Webster.

"Things are definitely looking up, up, UP," said Stink, telling himself a joke and cracking himself up, up, up.

* * *

Stink climbed on the bus. He held the Critter Keeper carefully in his lap. "Don't worry, Newton," said Stink. "I'll take really good care of you. The best."

"What's that?" asked Judy when she got on the bus.

"A red-spotted newt. Like a baby salamander. His name's Newton."

"Where'd you get him?"

"He's our class pet. We're studying life cycles, and Mrs. D. went to New Hamster and brought him back for us. I'm taking care of him for the weekend. I get to play with him and watch him and keep a journal of stuff that happens."

Judy snorted. "New *Hampshire,* Stink. Not New Hamster."

"You mean *Newt* Hampshire!" said Judy's friend Rocky.

"It's in *Newt* England," said Judy, cracking up. Stink rolled his eyes.

✳ ✳ ✳

When Stink got home, he did not stop to get a snack. Not even Fig *Newtons*. He took Newton up to his room. He got out his notebook and wrote:

friday 3:37 Newton hiding

Stink stared at the newt. Judy came in and peered over his shoulder.

friday 3:40 Newton hiding

friday 3:45 Newton still hiding

"You should write BORING in your journal," said Judy.

"Newts are not boring," said Stink.

"Name one UN-boring thing about a newt," said Judy.

"Newts eat crickets. And worms and slugs," said Stink.

"BOR-ing!" said Judy.

"Red-spotted newts are the state amphibian of New Hampshire."

"BOR-ing," said Judy.

"Okay. How about this? Newts start out as eggs. Then they hatch and swim around like tadpoles. Then they turn into red efts and live on land. Then they change color and go back to the water."

"Now that's a teensy-weensy bit not-boring," said Judy.

"And they shed their skins," Stink said.

"Interesting!" said Judy. "Call me when *that* happens."

* * *

On Saturday, Stink wrote in his journal some more.

10:52 Newton sniffed at worm
10:53 Newton sniffed at fake turtle
11:00 Newton ate cricket — whole!
11:30 Newton climbed up on new rock
11:36 Misted Newton with spray bottle
11:38 Newton stared at magazine picture of pond
11:45 Newton sleeping
12:00 Newton hiding
12:06 Still hiding

"Stink, are you going to stare at that newt all weekend?" asked Judy.

"I'm building him a raft. Out of Legos. Maybe he'll come out and float."

"You know what would be really UN-boring?" asked Judy. "Put the newt in with Toady."

"No way!" said Stink. "Newts are like poison to toads."

"So that means Toady won't eat him. C'mon, Stinker. Toady's all lonely." Before Stink could say Fig Newton, Judy scooped up Newton in her hands.

"You're supposed to wash your hands," said Stink. "Don't drop him."

"I won't drop him." She set him down on some moss in Toady's tank.

Newton sniffed at Toady and curled up his tail. "He's scared!" said Stink.

"Wait," said Judy. Toady licked Newton.

"Take him out!" yelled Stink.

"It was just a friendly lick," said Judy. "A newt lollipop."

"What if Toady gets poisoned? Get him out. Get him out!"

"Don't lay an egg!" Judy picked up Newton in her not-washed hand. "Stink! Something bad is wrong with Newton. His head is splitting open."

"Let me see!" Stink peered at the

newt. Sure enough, Newton's skin had split, starting right at his head.

"He's shedding his skin!" said Stink. "Put him back! Put him back!"

They peered at Newton. "Do you think it'll really come off?" asked Stink.

"Sure," said Judy. "It means he's growing. Unlike *some* people."

"Even a newt grows more than me," said Stink.

"BOR-ing. I wish something would happen," said Judy. She leaned over and wrote in Stink's journal:

1:15 Boring!

Stink erased it. "Growing takes time," he told Judy. "That's what everybody always tells me."

"Maybe if we say some magic words," said Judy.

> "Eye of newt,
> Blah blah blah,
> Wool of bat,
> Tongue of toad."

"It's happening!" said Stink.

"Rare!" said Judy. She ran to get the video camera. "Lights! Camera! Action!" Stink took out his journal and wrote:

1:10 Newton licked by a toad!

1:12 Newton gets splitting headache

1:21 Newton's skin falling off

1:35 Newton rubs against rock

1:39 Newton rubs against plant

1:44 Newton rubs against everything to shed skin

1:47 Newton's skin hanging by a thread

1:52 Newton bites off skin at tail!

"Gross!" said Judy. She stopped the camera.

"Sweet!" said Stink, staring at the newt skin.

"Hey, can I have it?" asked Judy. "To show my class, I mean?"

"No way!" said Stink. "You already showed the whole world my dried-up baby bellybutton. I'm showing *my* class."

"Mrs. Dumpster would want you to show my class, too."

"Not if you keep calling her Mrs. Dumpster."

Stink Moody stumbles upon a supersonic newt skin!

Stinkerbell, Shrinkerbell

P.U.! What's that smell?" Judy held her nose.

"What smell?"

"That dead-skunk smell. That one-hundred-year-old-dirty-sock smell. That three-hundred-year-old-rotten-egg smell." Judy walked around Stink's room, sniffing here, sniffing there. "It gets super-stinky as soon as you get close to Newton."

"Newton!" cried Stink. He sprang up from the floor, where he'd been drawing comics. Newton was in his hidey-hole. "Maybe it's the chopped-up dead worms in there. And dried-up crickets. Why isn't he eating?"

"Grody, grody, gross! There's green-y slime everywhere," Judy said.

"And brown stuff floating in the water."

"Stink, you have to clean it every day. Newts can die if their water gets too dirty."

"Since when are you the newt genius?"

"Since I read it in *Newtsweek*

magazine. You have to dump out the yucky water and wash the rocks and clean off all the slime and stuff."

"That's a lot of homework!" Stink said.

"C'mon, Stinkerbell. I'll help. We'll be the Slime Busters."

"Slime Busters! Double cool!" said Stink. "But you can't call me Stinkerbell."

"If you say so, Stinkerbell. Let's take it down to the big sink." Stink carried the Critter Keeper down to the kitchen, but he couldn't reach the sink.

"Here, let me," said Judy. She took

the Critter Keeper from Stink and set it on the counter. Stink stood on a kitchen chair.

"First we have to get Newton out so we can clean his house. Stink, hold this jar. Let's put Newton in there."

"Okay," said Stink, holding a tiny net. Judy reached in to scoop out Newton with her hand.

"The net!" cried Stink. "Mrs. D. says use the net for scooping him out."

"Hold on. Wait. I almost have him. Ha, ha!" said Judy. "Gotcha, you little newt-brain!"

"He is not a newt-brain," said Stink. "And . . . you're scaring him."

"He sure is slippery," said Judy. "You should call him Squirmy."

Just then, Squirmy squirmed right out of Judy's hand, slipped into the sink, and went *SLOOP!* right down the drain.

"Newton!" cried Stink. "You LOST him!" he yelled at Judy.

"Don't worry, Stink," said Judy. "He's probably just swimming around down there under the sink." Judy peered down the drain.

"Is he there?" asked Stink. "Do you see him?"

"I can't see," said Judy. "It's dark. . . . I need a flashlight or something. No. Wait. Let me turn the light on."

Judy flicked the switch over the sink. *GRRRRRRR!* A loud, grinding-up sound made them both jump back.

"STOP!" yelled Stink.

Judy turned off the switch. "Oops. Wrong switch."

"You killed Newton!" cried Stink. "The state amphibian of New Hampshire. My class pet. My homework!"

Stink ran to his room. He threw himself facedown on the bed.

Newton was gone. Gone, gon*er,* gon*est.* All that was left of Stink's class pet was his not-boring newt skin.

Stink gave the newt skin a place of honor on his desk. Right next to his gold Sacagawea dollar, his state quarters, and his French cootie catcher.

The newt skin just sat there. Lonely. Empty. Dead.

Deader than a doorknob.

Stink decided to do his homework. Homework always made him feel better.

Stink drew a still life of the newt skin for art class. He read a poem called "Who Has Seen the Wind?" He wrote one called "Who Has Seen the Newt?" and he used all his homework phrases in sentences.

Taking care of a newt is **easier said than done.**

I hope Newton does not get **cold feet** *out on the river.*

If your class pet goes down the drain, **go back to the drawing board.**

Judy came up to his room. "I'm sorry, Stink," she said. "I'm super-duper sorry. But I bet Newton slipped right down the pipes and on down to the river before I even flipped the switch."

Stink put down his pencil. "You think?"

"Newton is having the time of his

life. Think of it like *Stuart Little.* He's probably sailing down the river right now on a raft, having a big, fat, newt adventure."

"What am I going to tell Mrs. Dempster? And my class?"

"They'll understand. It's all part of the life cycle, Stink."

"The garbage disposal is NOT part of the life cycle!" said Stink.

Stink finished his homework. He wrote the last entry in his journal.

Sunday 5:21 NEWTON GOES DOWN THE DRAIN

The Famous Jameses

On Monday morning, when Stink told Mrs. D. about the G.D.I. (Garbage Disposal Incident), she said, "Let's just tell the class Newton ran away. It'll be our little secret." She wasn't even mad. She told Stink she was going back to New Hampshire for Presidents' Day weekend, and she could get another newt.

Class 2D wrote stories about the adventures they thought Newton was having in the big, wide world. Webster wrote about Newton joining a baseball team called the Newt York Yankees. Sophie of the Elves wrote about a magic kingdom where Princess Salamandra was under an evil spell and a newt in shining armor came to rescue her. And Stink wrote about Newton sailing down the river on a raft to Legoland and riding the roller coaster.

The stories made everybody feel much better. Especially Stink. Mrs. D.

even told Stink he could keep Newton's skin. As in, for real. For good. For*ever.*

✷ ✷ ✷

Mrs. Dempster talked about Presidents' Day for the rest of the week. Stink's class made cotton-ball portraits of George Washington. They made milk-carton-and-pretzel-stick log cabins in honor of Abraham Lincoln. Everybody said how tall Abe was. How tall his hat was. Tall, tall, tall. They acted like Abraham Lincoln was a giant.

"What's so great about living in a log cabin?" Stink asked Webster.

"Lincoln carved his math problems on the walls, right in the logs."

"He should have gotten in trouble for writing on the walls!" Stink said.

All week, nobody said a word about Stink's favorite president, James Madison. Not one peep. James Madison had a birthday, too. March 16.

Mrs. Dempster told the class, "Okay, 2D. Homework is on the board."

What does Presidents' Day mean to you?

"I know! I know!" said Calvin.

"Presidents' Day means you see flags."

"It means we don't have school on Monday," said Webster.

"It means you can buy stuff on sale, because presidents are on money," said Heather S.

"Let's not give away all our ideas," said Mrs. D. "I want everybody to write one page about what Presidents' Day means to *you*."

"Can we draw something, too?" asked Lucy.

"Can we write a poem?" asked Sophie of the Elves.

"Can we dress up?" asked Stink.

"Yes, yes, and yes," his teacher said. "But I still want my one page."

Stink took out his Big Head book of presidents. He flipped to the best president ever. President number four, James Madison.

Stink and James Madison were a lot alike. James Madison was from Virginia. Stink was from Virginia. James Madison had the name James. Stink had the name James! James Madison wore pants. Stink wore pants! Same-same!

More people should know about James Madison. They should have a statue of James Madison in the park. Or carve his head on the side of Mt. Trashmore. They should sing about him in the state song.

That gave Stink an idea. A great big Presidents' Day idea.

* * *

All the way home from school, Stink made up words for the state song. He sang it to the tune of *Frère Jacques*. He sang it for Mom. He sang it for Dad.

"Ja-ames Mad-i-son
Ja-ames Mad-i-son
Num-ber four, num-ber four
Changed his hair to white
Wrote the Bill of Rights
Ding, dang, dong
We love you."

"That's great!" said Mom. "I don't think we have a Virginia state song."

"There's a state bird. And a state flower," said Dad.

"And a Virginia state quarter," said Judy.

State quarter! Of course! Lincoln was on a penny. Washington was on a dollar. James Madison should be on the Virginia state quarter!

"Can I use your smelly markers?" Stink asked Judy.

"No," said Judy. "You never put the caps back on."

"Newton," said Stink. "N-E-W-T-O-N.

Poor little newt. *GRRRRRRR.*" Stink made a garbage disposal noise.

"Oh, go ahead," said Judy. "But that's IT. I'm not going to let you keep pulling a NEWTON on me!"

Stink sniffed a grape marker. He sniffed a blueberry marker. He sniffed a black licorice marker. *Yum, yum!*

He drew an outline of James Madison's head. On either side of it, he drew a quill pen and a number 4. Below it he wrote *E Pluribus Constitution.*

Then he wrote a letter to the governor.

Dear Mr. Governor:

You should make a James Madison Virginia state quarter. James Madison is way better than ships. Please tell me when you make the new quarter.

I am in second grade at Virginia Dare School. I have a bossy big sister and a cat named Mouse and I had a newt that reached the end of his life cycle.

Signed,

James E. Moody

P.S. Did you know you are governor of a state with no song?

The Adventures of Stink
in Newt in Shining Armor

BY STINK MOODY

Princess Salamandra is chased by the Evil Fly Dragon

I'm hungry!

MAGIC SPELL POPPY FIELD

...into the enchanted poppy field.

The princess falls into a deep sleep.

Now I've got you, Princess!

ZZZZZZ

NOT SO FAST!

It's Newt in shining armor! He has Fly Dragon's favorite food— Licorice!

YUM!

See you later, Fly Dragon!

Tumble, Fluff, Shrink!

om! Stink's doing homework again!" Judy said.

"You can't tell on me for doing homework," said Stink.

"Homework, schmome-work. Let's do something good."

"My homework's good."

"What's your homework?" asked Mom.

"Presidents' Day."

"You're not dressing up as a human flag again, are you?" asked Judy.

"No. I have to tell what Presidents' Day means to me."

"Stink, everybody knows what Presidents' Day means. Presidents' Day means your teacher reads you a book about George Washington's teeth and Abraham Lincoln's beard. Presidents' Day means you make stuff out of Popsicle sticks, like a log cabin or a flag."

"Nuh-uh," said Stink.

"Presidents' Day means you draw three circles. One for Lincoln, one for Washington, and one in the middle for the stuff that's the same about both."

"It's called a Venn diagram," Mom said.

"My homework is what it means to *me*. Not what it means to Mr. Venn."

"Good for you," Mom said. "What *does* Presidents' Day mean to *you*?"

"Two words," said Stink.

"Washington and Lincoln," said Judy.

"James Madison," said Stink.

Stink got out a bag of cotton balls. Stink made an old-timey James Madison wig. Judy helped him glue cotton balls to her old Brownie cap.

"Pass the glue," said Stink. "Quit hogging."

77

"Not so much!" said Judy. Stink didn't listen. He just kept gluing more cotton balls. "Let's see how it looks," said Stink.

"It has to dry first, or all the cotton balls will fall off," Judy told him.

"Let's dry it in the dryer, then," Stink said.

"Genius!" said Judy.

Stink put the wig in the dryer. "Press START," said Stink. "I can't reach."

Judy pressed the fluff-and-tumble button. They waited. *Ga-lump, ga-lump.* They waited some more. The buzzer went off. *"Voilà!"* said Judy, pulling out the wig.

"YIPES!" yelled Stink. "I said press START. Not SHRINK. Now it looks like . . . an elf wig. An *ant* wig."

"YOU put it in the dryer," said Judy.

"YOU pressed the button," said Stink.

"Never mind. We can put powder in your hair. Like James Madison."

"You mean *I* can put powder in my

hair," said Stink. "Just to make sure it doesn't turn orange or anything."

"BOR-ing," said Judy.

∗ ∗ ∗

On Friday, Webster read his report aloud first. It was about making red, white, and blue potholders at his grand-pa's nursing home on Presidents' Day.

"Presidents' Day means to me that we should have a girl president," said Sophie of the Elves. "Since we don't, I wrote a poem about a First Lady. Stink told me about her, and I found out more. Her name is Dolley Madison."

Dolley Madison, first to be called First Lady.

On a fifteen-cent stamp.

Liked to dance and fish and cook and ride horses.

Looked like a queen.

Easter egg hunt, started it.

Yum! Cupcakes are named for her.

Married James Madison.

Always won foot races.

Died in 1849.

Ice cream always dessert at the White House.

Saved a painting of George Washington from a fire.

Ostrich feathers in her hats.

Nice lady!

Last of all was Stink. He wore black. He pinned a number 4 to his shirt. He put white powder all over his hair.

WHAT PRESIDENTS' DAY
MEANS TO ME

by James Moody

James Madison was the shortest president ever. He was only five feet four inches tall, but he did great things.

Presidents' Day means we should not forget about the shortest president ever, James Madison. Everybody knows the tallest. But nobody knows the shortest. He was called 'little Apple-John.' They said he was 'no bigger than a half piece of soap.' That's a quote.

If you want to be president, it's good if your name is James. There are a lot of famous Jameses.

"Hey! Your real name is James, too," said Webster.

"Exactly." Stink grinned. He finished reading his report.

> *Six presidents had the name James, so it must be lucky. James Madison had the name James. He was smart. He wrote the Bill of Rights. He was Father of the Constitution.*
>
> *James Madison had eight brothers and sisters. If you're president, you get to boss even your big sister. He wore black. He put white powder in his hair to look older. He liked ice cream. He had a pet parrot. No lie. He loved science stuff, like*

the insides of rabbits. If James Madison was alive, he'd be over 250 years old.

My report is short because James Madison was short, too.

James Madison should be a quarter. James Madison should be a day off.

The End

The Adventures of Stink
in The Return of the Shrink Monster

by STINK MOODY

The Shrink Monster is back and he's MAD!

GRRRR!!

GULP!

What a headache!

He's about to throw Stink into the super-sonic clothes dryer to shrink him to nothing!

But Stink pushes the Monster into the dryer instead!

Stink pushes the button...

ON

He watches the monster SHRINK...

into a ball of lint!

President James Madison presents Stink with a medal and reward money!

$

Yay, Stink!

Tall, Taller, Tallest

It was Not-James-Madison-Day Monday. No school. Judy poked her head into Stink's room. "Stink, I'm supposed to be nice to you."

"Did Mom say?"

"Yep."

"Because of the newt?"

"Yep. And I'm supposed to make you feel taller or something. So, Stinkerbell, how about a birthday party?"

"A birthday party? For who?"

"Come downstairs and see."

Stink raced down the steps, two at a time.

Mom brought out twenty cupcakes on a big plate. They each had a letter on them, and all together, they spelled HAPPY JAMES MADISON DAY.

Dad lit the candles.

Everybody sang the James Madison State Song. Stink blew out all twenty candles. He ate an *M*, an *A*, and half of a *D*. Two and a half cupcakes!

"Presents!" said Judy.

"Presents? It's not even anybody's real birthday," said Stink.

"It's James Madison's un-birthday," said Judy.

"Dad and I made you a card," said Mom. "A Presidents' Day card."

"It was kind of short notice," said Dad. "So we printed some stuff off the Internet." Stink opened the card. It had pictures of short people.

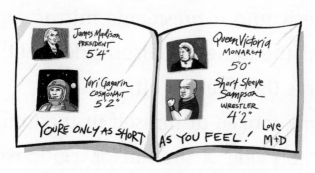

At the bottom of the card, Mom and Dad had printed in big letters:

YOU'RE ONLY AS SHORT AS YOU FEEL!

"I found the famous Wrestler Guy," said Judy.

"Thanks!" said Stink.

"Now mine," Judy said. Stink ripped it open. "It's a fun mirror!" Judy told him. "From Rocky's old magic kit. I made it into a presidents mirror. One side is the James Madison side and the other is the Abe Lincoln side."

Stink looked at himself in the James Madison side of the mirror. He looked super-shrimpy, and wide as a warthog. Everybody cracked up.

"Try the other side!" said Judy. Now

Stink looked skinny as a pencil and tall as Abe Lincoln.

"UN-Presidents' Day is better than Presidents' Day any time," said Stink. "WOW backward!"

"W-O-W backward is *wow*, too," said Judy.

"Exactly," said Stink.

"Thanks, you guys," said Stink. "For all the cupcakes and presents and stuff."

"The James Madison party was Judy's idea," said Dad.

"Yeah. Are you feeling any taller yet?" Judy asked.

"Maybe a little. Especially when I look in the Abe Lincoln mirror!"

"You know, you weren't always short," said Dad.

"Really?" asked Stink.

"Really?" asked Judy.

"You weren't short when you were a baby," said Mom. "You were long. Twenty-two inches long."

"What about me?" asked Judy.

"You were only about nineteen inches," said Dad.

"HA!" said Stink. "You mean *I* was taller than *Judy* when I was born?"

"I guess you could say that," said Mom.

"HA, HA!" Stink elbowed Judy. "Shorty Pants!"

"ROAR!" said Judy.

"More cupcakes, anyone?" Mom asked. "Oops. Almost forgot. An envelope came for you, Stink. Special delivery. Looks like it's from the governor." Mom handed Stink the envelope.

"Open it! Read it out loud!" said Judy.

Stink read the letter.

Dear Mr. James Moody,

Thank you kindly for your thoughts concerning the James Madison state quarter. Unfortunately, Virginia has already completed its state quarter program. We have no plans to issue another one at present. However, we do appreciate your enthusiasm for our forefather James Madison. Did you know that James Madison has been featured on a U.S. half dollar and also on a five-thousand-dollar bill?

Enclosed please find the James Madison Bronze Peace and Friendship Medal in honor of your interest in our fourth president.

Your Governor,
Jean MacDonald

"A five-thousand-dollar bill!" said Stink. "Double, triple, quadruple cool!"

The medal was a copper-colored coin in a plastic case. On one side it said *James Madison, President of the United States, 1809.* On the other, it had a picture of two hands shaking in friendship.

Stink passed around his brand-spanking-new James Madison friendship coin for everybody to see. While his family "oohed" and "aahed," Stink picked up the presidents mirror. He turned it to the tall side and looked at his reflection.

Everybody says growing takes time, thought Stink. *It's all part of the life cycle. One day, it's going to happen to me. Me! Mr. James Moody!*

Megan McDonald

is the author of the popular series starring Judy Moody. She says, "Once, while I was visiting a class, the kids chanted, 'Stink! Stink! Stink!' as I entered the room. In that moment, I knew that Stink had to have a book all his own." Megan McDonald lives in California.

Peter H. Reynolds ————————

is the illustrator of all the Judy Moody books. He says, "Stink reminds me of myself growing up: dealing with a sister prone to teasing and bossing around—and having to get creative in order to stand tall beside her." Peter H. Reynolds lives in Massachusetts.

Praise for
Stink: The Incredible Shrinking Kid

A Parents' Choice Recommended Title

"With child-savvy humor and energy, McDonald explores Stink's frustrations." —*Child*

"A welcome arrival for this age group."
—*Chicago Tribune*

"Judy Moody lovers (and their little brothers) will adore her younger brother, Stink."
—*Seattle Times*

"The narrative is fun and laced with puns . . . and it's peppered with black-and-white illustrations, including comics reflecting Stink's triumphant fantasies." —*Booklist*

"McDonald's breezy narrative and likable characters will keep Judy's followers amply amused and recruit new fans."
—*Publishers Weekly*

"Delightful full-page and spot-art cartoons and playful language in large type bring the child's adventures to life. 'Things are definitely looking up, up, UP' with this bright addition to beginning chapter-book collections."
—*School Library Journal*

"Stink definitely measures up to his memorable sister." —*Kirkus Reviews*

"McDonald cleverly pits Stink's earnest and slightly geeky personality against his sister's more adamant one, and she introduces some characters we hope to see more of."
—*Bulletin of the Center for Children's Books*

Check out Stink's next adventure!

Stink and the Incredible Super-Galactic Jawbreaker

Megan McDonald

illustrated by Peter H. Reynolds

Here's an excerpt. . . .

Stink took one lick. Then another. Then another. The giant jawbreaker was way too big to fit into his mouth.

Slurp. He licked that jawbreaker all the way home.

Sloop. He licked it all the way up to his room.

Slop. He licked it while he fed Toady one-handed. He licked it while he played with his president baseball cards (including James Madison, thanks to Judy). He licked it while he did his homework one-handed.

He even licked it while he set the table for dinner. One-handed, of course.

Pretty soon his lips were green and his tongue was blue and his hands were as sticky as gum on a sneaker bottom.

"Hey," Judy asked at dinner. "Why is there a big fat sticky blue fingerprint on my plate?"

"Oops," said Stink, licking off his fingers. "Finger-lickin' good!"

"Stink's eating a jawbreaker for dinner!" said Judy, pointing.

An excerpt from *Stink and the Incredible Super-Galactic Jawbreaker*

"Stink, put that jawbreaker down and eat some real food," said Dad. "Here. Have some macaroni."

"This *is* real food," said Stink. "It contains vitamins A and C and calcium. No lie."

"And dextrose, sucrose, fructose, and other stuff that makes you comatose," said Judy.

"It's NOT going to make me comb my toes," said Stink.

"And don't forget wax," said Judy.

"Macaroni," said Mom. "You heard Dad. And green beans."

"But it didn't break my jaw yet,"

said Stink. "It didn't even stretch my mouth one bit."

"You already have a big mouth," said Judy.

"Hardee-har-har," said Stink. "Well, it didn't set my tongue on fire yet or make my cheeks feel like a chipmunk, either."

"It may not break your jaw," said Judy, "but all your teeth are going to fall out. For sure and absolute positive. Did you know Queen Elizabeth ate so many candies from her pockets that her teeth turned black? No lie!"

DOUBLE RARE!
Judy Moody has her own website!

Come visit **www.judymoody.com**
for the latest in all things Judy Moody, including:

- ❂ All you need to know about the best-ever
  Judy Moody Fan Club

- ❂ Answers to all your V.I.Q.s (very important
  questions) about Judy

- ❂ Way-not-boring stuff about Megan McDonald
  and Peter H. Reynolds

- ❂ Double-cool activities that will be sure to put you
  in a mood—and not a bad mood, a good mood!

- ❂ Totally awesome T.P. Club info!

Judy MOODY

Was in a mood. Not a good mood. A bad mood.

Megan McDonald   illustrated by Peter H. Reynolds

Judy MOODY Gets Famous!

Megan McDonald   illustrated by Peter H. Reynolds

Judy MOODY Saves the World!

Megan McDonald   illustrated by Peter H. Reynolds

Judy MOODY Predicts the Future

Megan McDonald   illustrated by Peter H. Reynolds

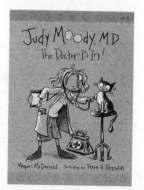

Judy MOODY, M.D. The Doctor IS In!

Megan McDonald   illustrated by Peter H. Reynolds

★ Judy MOODY ★ Declares Independence

Megan McDonald   illustrated by Peter H. Reynolds

Judy MOODY's

INCLUDES 24 STICKERS INSIDE!

Double-Rare Way-Not-Boring Book of Fun Stuff to Do

Megan McDonald   illustrated by Peter H. Reynolds

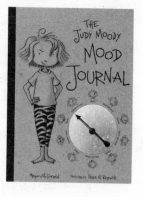

THE JUDY MOODY MOOD JOURNAL

Megan McDonald   illustrated by Peter H. Reynolds

Experience
all of
Judy Moody's
moods!

Don't forget
Stink's
big sister....

"I can have moods too, you know."
Stink kept counting. "One hundred
eighteen, one hundred nineteen . . ."

"Is it because your jawbreaker's all
gone?" asked Judy.

"It's because that jawbreaker lied.
They should call it World's Biggest
UN-jawbreaker. I ate and ate that
thing for one whole week, and it did
not break my jaw. Not once. It didn't
even make my mouth one teeny-
weeny bit bigger."

Then, in one single bite, one not-jaw-breaking crunch, it was G-O-N-E, gone.

Stink was down in the dumps. He moped around the house for one whole day and a night. He stomped up the stairs. He stomped down. He drew comics. *Ka-POW!* He did not play with Toady once. He did not do his homework. He went outside and bounced Judy's basketball 117 times.

"Somebody got up on the WRONG side of the bed," said Judy. "If I didn't know better, I'd think you were in a MOOD."

Stink's jawbreaker went from super-galactic to just plain galactic. From golf-ball size to Super-Ball size.

"Are you still eating that thing?" asked Judy. Stink stuck out his tongue.

"Well, you look like a skink," said Judy. She pointed to his blue tongue.

Shloop! went Stink.

Stink ate his not-super-galactic jawbreaker for one whole week. He ate it when it tasted like chalk. He ate it when it tasted like grapefruit. He ate it through the fiery core to the sweet, sugary center. He ate it down to a marble. A teeny-tiny pea.

An excerpt from *Stink and the Incredible Super-Galactic Jawbreaker*

"At least I won't have to brush them every day!" said Stink.

* * *

Every day, Stink ate a little more and a little more of his jawbreaker. He ate it in bed first thing in the morning before he brushed his teeth. He ate it at recess in between playing H-O-R-S-E with his super-duper best friend, Webster. He ate it on the bus and all the way home from school.

He gave a lick to Mouse the cat. He gave a lick to Toady the toad. He even tried giving a lick to Jaws the Venus flytrap.

An excerpt from *Stink and the Incredible Super-Galactic Jawbreaker*